⇥ *Myrna Never Sleeps* ⇤

Myrna Never Sleeps

➤ ❧

by Beth Peterson

illustrated by John O'Brien

ATHENEUM BOOKS FOR YOUNG READERS

Atheneum Books for Young Readers
An imprint of Simon & Schuster Children's Publishing Division
1230 Avenue of the Americas
New York, NY 10020

Designed by Laura Hammond Hough
The text of this book is set in Adobe Caslon.
The illustrations were done in pen and ink.

Manufactured in the United States of America
10 9 8 7 6 5 4 3 2 1

Library of Congress Cataloging-in-Publication Data
Peterson, Beth.
    Myrna never sleeps / by Beth Peterson ; illustrated by John O'Brien. —1st ed.
        p.   cm.
    Summary: Putting out a forest fire, saving kidnapped cats, finding lost trea-
sure, and rescuing survivors of a storm keep a youg girl from going to sleep.
    ISBN 0-689-31893-6
    [1. Bedtime—Fiction.   2. Imagination—Fiction.   3. Adventure and advetur-
ers—Fiction.]   I. O'Brien, John (John Edward Thomas), ill.   II. Title.
PZ7.P44324My   1995
[Fic]—dc20   93-8301

For Marcy,
who has been known to keep late hours

→ *C*ontents ←

✦ Myrna Never Sleeps ✦

Blazing Disasters

*M*yrna never sleeps, or so it seems. When the lights go out and the door closes quietly behind her mother, she lies in bed with her eyes wide open. Sometimes a full moon peeks around the clouds, and the sound of distant traffic drifts in an open window.

One night an owl began hooting nearby. Myrna knew the owl was a dispatcher for the bird grapevine, so she listened very carefully.

The message was unmistakable. A forest fire was raging out of control! All the animals were fleeing from the flames, dashing desperately for safety. Hearing their cries, Myrna sprang from her bed and grabbed her fire-fighting gear. Dashing to the bathroom, she hooked up her special fire-fighting hose to the sink. This was her very special hose that can stretch for miles and miles and is so lightweight it is no problem at all to carry.

In a flash she was out the window and sliding down the roof. As always when on a mission like this, Myrna could leap fences effortlessly and attain speeds unknown in official racing records. If you had been there, all you'd have seen was a blur of movement passing so fast you'd have wondered if you'd seen anything at all.

Leaving the houses and highways

behind, she headed into the hills, deftly skirting trees and bushes as she pushed on toward the roaring fire. A fox sped past her, going in the opposite direction. Then squirrels and elk and deer passed her. A large black bear ran by on all fours, galloping down the hill.

"Run!" they cried. "Run for your life!"

Fearlessly Myrna advanced toward the fire. She was not unfamiliar with calamities and disasters. Why, just the other night she had traveled as far as Peru to rescue an entire village after an earthquake. And the week before she'd been on the scene of a very violent volcanic eruption in Alaska. She was widely respected in some quarters for her disaster expertise.

As she neared the scene of the fire, she could hear cries for help all around. The smoke grew so thick it was hard to see, and she was glad she had remembered to bring her fire goggles.

Under a fallen tree, she found a rabbit trembling with fear and reached down to pick it up. Just as she was tucking it into her jacket for safekeeping, a large flame leaped up at her feet. Myrna stomped on the flame vigorously with her thick fire boots until it was gone.

As more flames darted up around her, she took aim with the special hose and turned the nozzle. Like the most powerful fountain in the world, water gushed forth high into the air. It spread out and fell in a great flood on the burning trees and fleeing animals. Some of the animals got a little wet, but they didn't mind because it was so very hot with all the smoke and fire.

A raccoon stumbled out from the trees ahead, panting and gasping for air.

"It's a furnace in there. A furnace!" he said, choking.

Myrna bent down to give the raccoon a drink from the hose.

"Thanks," said the raccoon, wiping his mouth. He stumbled past her, heading away

from the blazing forest. "Get away while you can!" he called back to Myrna.

Myrna knew she couldn't take the raccoon's advice, wise as it might be. Her very important mission to save the forest naturally overcame any concern for mere personal safety.

She advanced on the fire, swinging the hose in every direction. Burning boughs crackled overhead, and thick billows of smoke blew across the treetops. Flames darted at her and retreated as the water drenched everything in sight. Staunchly, Myrna held her ground until the fire began to sizzle and sputter and slowly go out.

Tucking the hose under her arm, Myrna wiped her brow with her sleeve and surveyed her night's work. The smoke was gone. She had arrived just in time to prevent serious damage. Some of the trees had lovely green leaves still clinging to their branches, though they were a bit wet. She took the little rabbit out of her jacket and set it on the ground as the other animals returned and gathered around her. One by one they approached her and shook her hand.

"Thank you, Myrna, Firefighter Supreme," said the fox, bowing deeply in her honor.

"Myrna the Magnificent!" cried the little rabbit.

"We can't thank you enough," said the elk. "You were stupendously wonderful."

"Good job," said the bear, nearly knocking her over as he patted her heartily on the back.

"Hey, those are great goggles," said the wolf. "I could use a pair like that."

Myrna took off her goggles and handed them to the wolf.

"Please keep them," she said. "I can get another pair."

"Wow. Thanks a lot," said the wolf as he put on the goggles. He waved good-bye and trotted off into the forest to look for his friends.

Myrna shook hands and exchanged pleasantries with the last of the returning animals. Then she waved good-bye to everyone and raced home at top speed to await word of any more cataclysmic calamities, dreadful disasters, or miscellaneous misfortunes that might require her expert assistance. She climbed back in the window just as someone knocked on the bathroom door.

"Myrna, is that you?" asked her mother.

"Yes, it's me," said Myrna.

Her mother opened the door.

"You should be in bed," she said, glancing around the room. "How did you manage to get water all over everything?"

"Well," said Myrna poking her toe at a big puddle near her feet. "There was a forest fire."

"In the bathroom?" asked her mother.

"Well," said Myrna slowly, looking a little sheepish.

"Come on, back to bed," said her mother, picking up a stuffed animal with swimming goggles fastened around its head.

→ 2 ←

Cats in Jeopardy

$\mathcal{M}$yrna climbed back into bed, and her mother tucked the blankets up to her chin. Outside the window, the big moon was still playing hide-and-seek with the scurrying clouds.

"No more getting up," said her mother. "I want you to go to sleep."

"I'll try," said Myrna as her mother closed the door.

Myrna closed her eyes, and they popped

right open. She closed them again, and they popped open again. She closed them once more, and her cat, Squeal, jumped up on the bed.

"Yeeooww," said Squeal as Myrna's eyes opened wide.

"What is it, Squeal?" asked Myrna.

"Yeeooww," Squeal repeated.

Myrna sat straight up in bed.

"Oh no! That's terrible," she said.

Somebody was kidnapping cats. Yes! Kidnapping cats! They were taking them off porches and fences and windowsills. They were gathering them up from alleys and yards and taking them away to a cat circus where they would be forced to wear silly clothes and perform stupid tricks.

Myrna knew how much cats hate to wear silly clothes and do stupid tricks. Several times Squeal had made quite a point of just how much he hated such things. She threw off the blankets and sprang out of bed.

"Don't worry, Squeal," she said as she grabbed her trench coat and donned her baseball cap. "I'll save them!"

Myrna dashed for her custom-made detecting van, specially equipped with radio receivers to pick up signals from near and far. As she sped down the street, she turned the dial on the radio until she found the catnappers' frequency. A voice came over the airwaves.

"Hey, Howard, I just spotted a tabby on a porch on Flea Street. Looks like just the one we need to round out tonight's catch."

"Go for it, Herb," said the catnapper named Howard. "I'll meet you back at headquarters."

"Will do. Ten-four," replied Herb.

Myrna screeched around a corner on two wheels. Squeal, who had come along to help, nearly fell off his seat.

"Put your seat belt on, Squeal!" yelled Myrna as she screeched around another corner onto Flea Street. Up ahead she saw an old, beat-up truck pulling away from her friend Becky's house. Through the back window of the truck she could see numerous cat faces pressed against the glass, mouths opened in soundless meows.

"They got Becky's cat! We must stop them, Squeal," Myrna said, stepping on the gas. The catnapper called Herb must have stepped on the gas, too, for the truck sped away and turned onto the highway leading out of town.

Myrna took another corner on two wheels and raced onto the highway. In the distance, she could see the truck's taillights on the dimly lit road. Suddenly, the lights disappeared. Frantically, Myrna turned the radio dial, trying to pick up the catnappers' signal, but the airwaves were silent. She drove along the highway, peering down side streets for any trace of the truck.

"We've got to find them," she said to Squeal, who was leaning up on the dashboard with his paws, watching the road ahead. "We've got to save all those poor cats from a fate worse even than death."

The radio suddenly sputtered and crackled. "Hey, Howard," said Herb. "I gotta make a stop."

"What for?" asked Howard.

"I'm hungry," said Herb. "I'm gonna stop for a quick bite at the Nightbird Café."

"Okay, but don't dawdle," said Howard.

"Ten-four," said Herb.

Myrna knew the Nightbird Café well. A few of her previous cases had taken her to the drab little diner with its grimy windows and peeling paint. It was a notorious hangout for catnappers, dog snatchers, horse heisters, swine swipers, ferret filchers, peafowl poachers, stoat stealers, raccoon raiders, and bird abductors.

Myrna turned the van carefully into the parking lot, shutting off the powerful, night-piercing headlights. In the dark, they rolled up quietly beside Herb's truck.

"What luck," said Myrna to Squeal. "He's already inside, filling his face. Let's go."

They slid silently out of their seats and opened the back of the van. Then they crept to the catnappers' truck and carefully opened the back doors.

"Oh, Myrna!" cried the cats. "We're so happy to see you!"

"Shhhh!" said Myrna. "Quick! Run for the van and keep it quiet."

The cats leaped out of the truck, streaking by Myrna's feet with tails flying every which way. House cats and barn cats and alley cats and show cats, cool cats and hepcats and tomcats and mousers darted for the safety of Myrna's van. When the last cat had squeezed in, Myrna secured the back doors. Just as she and Squeal were climbing into the front seat, Herb came running out of the Nightbird Café.

"Stop," he yelled as Myrna backed out, tires screaming, and spun the van around.

"I'll get you!" he shouted, waving a fist at Myrna as he jumped in his truck.

The van flew down the highway with Herb close on its tail. Myrna knew her special detecting van was more than a match for any car or truck. The dash was decorated with dozens of medals she had won at all the major racing events in the world.

"Hang on, Squeal!" she hissed between gritted teeth.

The van and truck zigzagged along the dark, twisting highway, weaving dangerously around sharp curves. With steady hands and steely nerves, Myrna kept to the road, though sometimes just barely. As the truck steadily gained on her, she knew she would have to resort to more extreme measures to get rid of it. She waited until the truck was close enough to see Herb's angry red face in the mirror. Then she reached down and pressed the secret turbo button. Faster than a streak of lightning, the van shot down the highway, leaving Herb choking in a cloud of dust.

"Yeah, Myrna!" shouted all the cats in delight. "Way to go, Myrna!"

"Myrna, Ace Detective!" yelled a tailless Manx.

"The Peerless Private Eye!" added a pug-nosed Persian.

"And Singular Sleuth!" chimed a sleek Siamese.

"We are forever in your debt," exclaimed a skinny, hairless Sphynx. "How can we ever repay you?"

Myrna blushed. "It's nothing, really," she said. Then she kindly offered to take each cat home.

"Drop me off at the alley behind Dan's Dirty Dog Saloon," said a scruffy gray tabby.

"I'll get off at the corner of Kitty Litter Lane," said a black Bombay cat.

"The north side of Pekingese Park will do for me," called a yellow cat with scars on its ears.

"Kindly let me out at Anne's Ancient Antiques and Cat Collectibles," a plump Burmese politely requested.

Myrna drove back and forth all around town while Squeal consulted the road map. After seeing Becky's cat safely back to its porch and making one more stop at Fannie Feline's Finishing School, Myrna headed the van toward home.

She and Squeal were carefully turning the radio dial, listening for distress signals, when the door to Myrna's room opened.

"Okay, back to bed," said her mother, coming into the room. "It's much too late to be listening to the radio."

Myrna got up from where she'd been kneeling next to the clock radio on her night table. Squeal jumped off the table and disappeared into the closet, where he made a careful count of all Myrna's shoes and discarded socks.

"Sorry, Mom," Myrna said, taking off her baseball cap.

"I'll take the coat, too, please," said her mother, holding out her hand.

Myrna took off her mother's tan raincoat with the detectivelike flaps on the shoulders and handed it to her.

"Squeal and I had to rescue some cats," she explained as she climbed back into bed. "Horrible catnappers were stealing all the cats in town."

"Well, we can make a full report to the police in the morning," her mother said. "Right now I want you to go to sleep."

"Okay, Mom," Myrna said. "I'll try."

✦ 3 ✦

Regions Unknown

*T*he clouds outside had swollen in size and nearly hid the moon as they wove themselves into a dark blanket across the sky. Myrna's mother closed the window and tucked Myrna in before turning out the lights and leaving the room. Rain pattered against the window. Squeal reappeared and sat on the sill, watching the water run down on the other side of the glass. A passenger plane rumbled by dimly in the night sky.

Myrna looked out the window from her first-class reserved seat at the earth passing below. The plane was heading south, far south, as she set out on another trek to explore regions unknown.

"Say, aren't you Myrna, the World Renowned Explorer of Regions Unknown?" asked the stewardess as she handed Myrna a cup of steaming hot chocolate with melted marshmallows floating on top.

Myrna nodded.

Some of the passengers turned to look at her and smile, thrilled at sharing a plane with an international celebrity.

"Where are you headed for? Got any special plans?" asked one of the passengers.

"Well, I really can't tell you," said Myrna. "These things are top secret until the discoveries are made."

The plane set down in a distant city. Myrna had to take first a cab, then a bus, then a train, and then another bus before setting out on foot. Hiking over wooded hills and through lush valleys, she stopped now and then to check the secret map she had drawn up after many years of research in all the libraries of Europe. Her destination would take her far from civilization, to a spot in the middle of the map that she had marked with a gold star.

Forging deeper into the wild heartland, she cut a trail through tangled jungles and waded knee-deep through dank swamps. Long-tailed monkeys and flashy macaws jabbered and squawked at her as she passed. Stepping gingerly on slippery rocks to cross a stream, she made it safely to the other side before one of the rocks moved and turned and looked up at her out of big crocodile eyes.

When she happened unexpectedly upon a village, Myrna stopped to visit for a while. She drank some very sugary tea she was kindly offered and, in turn, passed around her tin of assorted cookies and a bag of lemon drops. She and the villagers exchanged small talk about the local scenery, the mild weather, and the soaring price of good shoes. Then, waving a hearty good-bye, Myrna left to continue on her expedition.

Finally, late that night, Myrna reached her secret destination—a high flatland deep in the undiscovered mountains of an as yet unnamed country. Her research had proved exactly right, and before her lay the Lost City of Antiquity, glowing peacefully in the moonlight.

"Rats!" said Myrna as she realized she was not the only one to discover the Lost City. Two shadowy figures were digging away on the other side of the ruins.

Quietly, she crept closer and hid behind a crumbling wall. Bats flitted silently overhead while furry little rodents scurried unseen among the fallen stones. The two diggers were so busy they didn't notice Myrna, but she recognized them.

"The scoundrels!" she hissed under her breath, for they were the very same men who had sat behind her at the great library in Paris, trying to see over her shoulder to read her map.

The scoundrels were digging up the treasures of the Lost City and throwing them in sacks. Myrna knew they planned to take the treasures and sell them and become very rich. When they were done digging, they shouldered their sacks and turned to leave.

Myrna slipped silently ahead of them through the shadowy ruins. She had to find a way to stop them before they got away. Behind her she could hear the men talking loudly and laughing at how rich they would soon be.

"Not if I can help it!" Myrna declared in a whisper.

Working quickly, she drew some string out of her knapsack and fastened it at ankle level between two trees. Then she hid again as the thieves approached, still laughing and bragging.

"Gold! Gold! Lovely, lovely gold!" sang one of the men, who began laughing and punching the other one playfully on the arm.

"We'll be rich, filthy rich!" sang the other thief.

Myrna smiled to herself. The villainous, scoundrelly rogues were walking right into her trap.

"What the . . . !" yelled one of the rogues as the string caught both their ankles and sent them headlong to the ground.

Myrna sprang from her hiding place and snatched the sacks full of treasure. She jumped right over the sprawled bodies of the thieves and raced down the trail from the high plateau of the Lost City. Behind her the thieves had scrambled to their feet and were running after her, yelling and shouting and calling her very unpleasant names.

Panting and out of breath, Myrna reached the village she had passed on the way up. The villagers ran out of their houses to see what was wrong.

"We must hide the treasure before the thieves get here!" she cried.

The villagers hustled Myrna and the treasure into a storeroom and buried her under some flour sacks. When the thieves arrived and asked if anyone had seen a girl run by, they all shook their heads and stared blankly, pretending not to understand. The thieves left in frustration and disappeared down the trail, still looking for Myrna.

Myrna and the villagers all laughed and patted each other on the back. The thieves could go on searching forever, but they'd never find Myrna, and their pockets would remain just as empty as they were before.

"What should we do with the treasure of the Lost City?" asked Myrna.

"Lost City?" said one of the villagers. "It's not a lost city."

"We've known about it all along," said another villager. "We just didn't tell anyone."

"We wanted to keep it a secret," said a third one. "We didn't want lots of tourists coming up here and tramping all over our vegetable gardens."

"Oh dear," said Myrna. "I didn't know. I'm sorry I found it and ruined the secret."

"Well, that's okay. It was bound to happen sometime," said the first villager. "I guess we better build a museum for all the treasure."

Myrna helped the villagers build a museum. They made some very nice shelves and arranged all the lovely little gold statues and gem-studded jewelry for display. Myrna was so busy chatting and arranging that she didn't notice anyone behind her until someone tapped her on the shoulder. She turned

around to see her mother standing behind her, arms folded and looking a little tired.

"Myrna," her mother said. "I hope this is the last time I have to put you to bed tonight. You can rearrange your shelves tomorrow."

"I'm sorry, Mom," said Myrna, setting a china dog back on the shelf. "But how can I sleep when I'm not even tired?"

"You'll just have to try," replied her mother. "Fighting fires and rescuing cats should be enough to tire anyone."

"And finding lost treasure," whispered Myrna, not a bit tired.

⇾ 4 ⇽

The High Seas

*M*yrna's mother tucked her in one more time and left the room. A branch knocked against the side of the house and streams of water slid down the window as the clouds burst in a torrent of lashing rain. Squeal had disappeared from the sill and was safely curled up under the bed.

Myrna closed her eyes. She had just taken a bite of the poisoned apple forced on her by the cruel old hag and now would have to lie sleeplike until kissed by an ugly frog. She hoped the frog would hurry, because she was having a hard time keeping her eyes closed.

Lightning flared in the sky outside, and thunder rolled over the rooftops. Between peals of thunder, Myrna heard the cries of her baby brother, Michael. He had been crossing Catfish Creek when the rising storm knocked out the bridge, sending Michael tumbling into the floodwaters below.

"I'm coming, Michael! I'm coming!" she cried.

Myrna jumped into the Amazing Boatcar and quickly pressed the button marked Dry Land. Wheels emerged from the bottom and the motor roared to life as another peal of thunder rocked the sky. The driving rain and fierce winds nearly forced her off the road as she headed for the swollen banks of Catfish Creek.

At the creek's edge, Myrna jabbed the High Seas button and plunged into the turbulent water as the wheels were replaced by a rudder and a powerful outboard motor popped into place behind her. The nose of the Boatcar tilted high in the air as Myrna raced along the creek, searching the waters and calling Michael's name.

Up ahead she spotted a little brown head bobbing with the current and little arms flailing at the water.

"Hang on, Michael!" she cried, wiggling quickly into her wet suit and fastening her flippers. She grabbed her oxygen tank, secured it in place, and jumped overboard.

The creek had swollen to the size of a river, and Myrna had to fight gigantic waves

whipped up by the storm. She dived deep beneath the surface, so deep she could see hundreds of catfish huddled on the bottom of the creek, hiding from all the turmoil above. She swam on until she recognized Michael's kicking legs amid the broken branches and discarded junk swirling around on the surface. Myrna pushed off from the bottom of the creek and jetted up out of the water right alongside her brother.

"Grab onto the oxygen tank," she instructed Michael, who was so glad to see her that for once he did as she asked.

Myrna battled the current upstream until they came to the Boatcar, which she had secured firmly in place with a huge anchor before jumping overboard. They climbed in, hauled up the anchor, and turned the Boatcar around.

The current was fast and fierce as they fought their way upstream. A floating branch hit the side of the Boatcar, and a water rat scrambled from it and jumped in.

"Whew! What a storm, eh?" said the water rat. "Thanks for the lift." He shook the

water from his back and settled comfortably into a corner.

A brown, long-eared puppy came swirling toward them, clinging to a broken plank. Myrna and Michael both reached over the side and hauled the puppy in. Then they

saw a duck swimming frantically in circles and squawking, trying not to get hit by all the bits of rubbish washed down by the storm.

"Over here!" they called to the duck. The duck swam over to the Boatcar and gratefully climbed inside.

"Oh, thank you so much," said the duck. "A bird could get seriously injured, what with all that garbage floating around," she added as she smoothed her feathers.

They rescued an otter and an opossum, a weasel and a woodchuck, a frog and a ferret, and a kangaroo that had been visiting from Australia. A whole family of beavers, whose home had been washed away when the dam broke, waved at them from a log in the middle of the stream. They pulled up alongside and helped all the little beavers climb in.

When a shark swam over and circled

the Boatcar, Myrna and Michael and the animals agreed that it would not be a good idea to invite it in. It was probably hungry, since sharks are always hungry, and everyone knows you never invite a hungry shark into your boat. They are not picky eaters.

The Boatcar was so loaded down with soggy, wet passengers that they just barely made it to shore. Michael passed around towels and blankets while Myrna switched to Dry Land mode. Branches swayed darkly in the wind and rain beat against the windshield as she guided them through the storm.

When they got home, Myrna suggested they have a Storm Survivors Party. She tried to convince Michael that it was only appropriate that they should open his box of animal crackers and share them with their animal guests. Michael had his doubts about this and held the box of crackers tightly in his hands until Myrna pointed out that the little puppy really looked very hungry and the baby beavers hadn't eaten for days. So Michael opened the box and passed the crackers around.

Everyone got two crackers, and they all sat in a circle telling stories as they munched. Outside the wind howled around the house, but inside everyone was cozy and happy. They laughed and joked and sighed at their adventure on the high seas of Catfish Creek until late into the night.

→ ←

When Myrna's mom opened the door to Myrna's room the next morning, she stood in the doorway shaking her head.

"That girl never sleeps," she said to herself as she passed Myrna's empty bed to open the window.

The sun had been up for hours, warming the wet rooftops and sodden lawns. Bits of broken branches littered the driveways, and a phone line had come down in the storm. A crew from the phone company was busily repairing the line.

Myrna's mom walked softly down the hall to Michael's room and peeked in. Beneath the window, the sun ran over Michael's empty bed. She started to enter the room and nearly tripped on a pair of bright green flippers and a pink plastic snorkel lying at her feet. Myrna's mom sighed.

A mass of blankets and towels and pillows were piled on the floor. All Michael's stuffed animals were neatly set out in a circle

around the heap. In the middle of all this, curled up close and surrounded by pillows, lay Myrna and Michael fast asleep.

Myrna's mom righted a little brown kangaroo that had fallen on its side and picked up an empty box of animal crackers. She left the room, closing the door quietly behind her.